This edition published by Parragon Books Ltd in 2016

Parragon Books Ltd
Chartist House
15–17 Trim Street
Bath BA1 1HA, UK
www.parragon.com

Adapted by Samantha Crockford
Illustrated by the Disney Storybook Artists
Designed by Sophie Willcox
Production by Charlene Vaughan

ISBN 978-1-4748-2787-4

Printed in China

DISNEY
ZOOTROPOLIS

PaRragon

Bath · New York · Cologne · Melbourne · Delhi
Hong Kong · Shenzhen · Singapore · Amsterdam

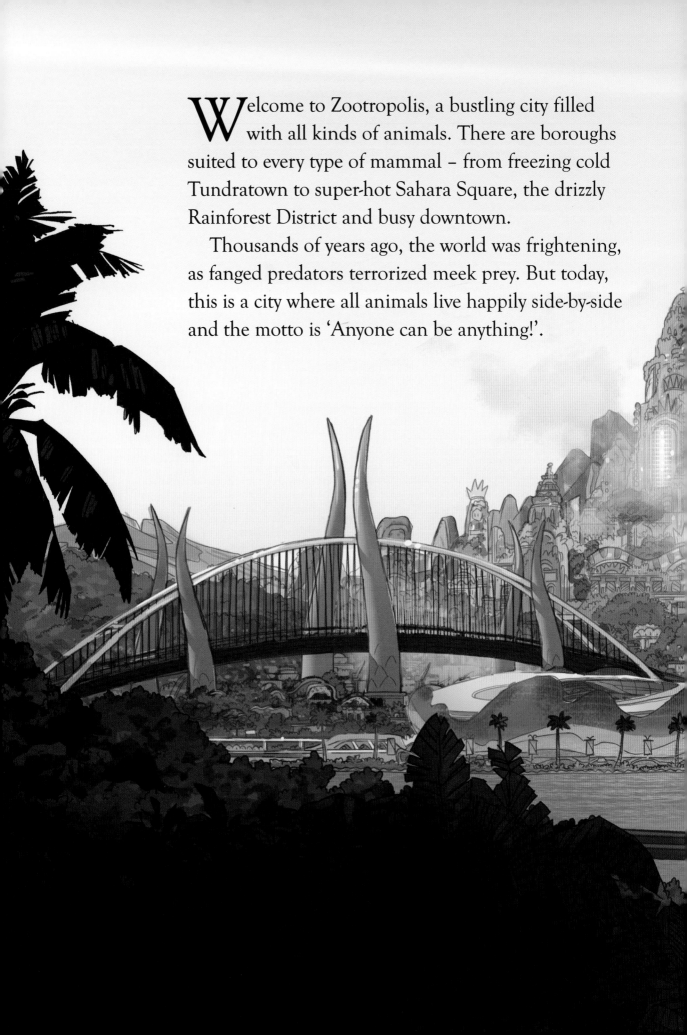

Welcome to Zootropolis, a bustling city filled with all kinds of animals. There are boroughs suited to every type of mammal – from freezing cold Tundratown to super-hot Sahara Square, the drizzly Rainforest District and busy downtown.

Thousands of years ago, the world was frightening, as fanged predators terrorized meek prey. But today, this is a city where all animals live happily side-by-side and the motto is 'Anyone can be anything!'.

On the outskirts of the city, in Bunnyburrow, little Judy Hopps believed in the city's motto with all her heart. At her local talent show, she happily announced that she wanted to be a police officer in the ZPD (the Zootropolis Police Department) when she grew up.

Where anyone can be anything

Later that day, Judy overheard a nasty snarl.

"Gimme your tickets, you meek little sheep!"

A mean fox named Gideon Grey was bullying some of the other kids into handing over their Carrot Days Festival tickets. Judy raced to defend her friends, but Gideon pushed her to the ground.

"Too bad no dumb bunny ain't never gonna be a cop!" he teased.

The bully walked away laughing, not realizing that Judy had taken the tickets back when he wasn't looking!

Judy never gave up on her dream to become a police officer. When she was old enough, she went to the Police Academy and worked harder than anybody else. She finished at the top of her class!

She left her family in Bunnyburrow and moved to the centre of Zootropolis to become the first ever bunny police officer in the ZPD. She couldn't believe it – this place was amazing! The city was built so that each animal, no matter how large or small, could move around easily.

On her first day at work, Judy was surrounded by animals much larger than her. But nothing could dampen her enthusiasm and she paid careful attention as Chief Bogo explained the day's assignments.

"We have fourteen missing mammal cases, more than we've ever had," Bogo said. Then one by one, he handed out the cases to various officers. When it came to Judy, though, the assignment was different. "Parking duty!" he barked.

Judy felt disappointed. She wanted real police work, not parking duty. Still, she was determined to make the most of her job. Using her excellent bunny hearing, she could hear the *ding* of expired parking metres from streets away. By lunchtime, she had ticketed more than 200 cars!

Suddenly, a movement caught her eye. Judy saw a fox pause and look around as he entered an ice cream shop. Judy thought his behaviour seemed suspicious, and foxes could be sly animals, so she crossed the street to follow him.

Jumbeaux's Café was filled with huge animals buying huge dishes of ice cream. Judy spotted the fox and was surprised to learn he was just trying to buy a Jumbo-pop for his son, who loved everything about elephants and was even dressed in an elephant costume.

"There aren't any fox ice cream joints in your part of town?" the elephant behind the counter, Jerry, asked.

Judy didn't like to see any animal treated this way, so she quickly stepped forward, showed her ZPD badge and convinced Jerry to serve the fox and his son.

Jerry finally agreed to sell them a Jumbo-pop, but then the fox realized that he had forgotten his wallet! Judy told him it was no problem and paid for the Jumbo-pop herself.

On the pavement outside, the fox turned to Judy.

"Officer," he said. "I really can't thank you enough. So kind, really. Can I pay you back?"

"Oh no, my treat," Judy replied, then introduced herself.

The fox told her his name. "Wilde. Nick Wilde."

Judy leaned down to Nick's son. "If you want to be an elephant when you grow up, you be an elephant," she told the little fox, "because this is Zootropolis. Anyone can be anything."

With that, Judy and Nick went their separate ways.

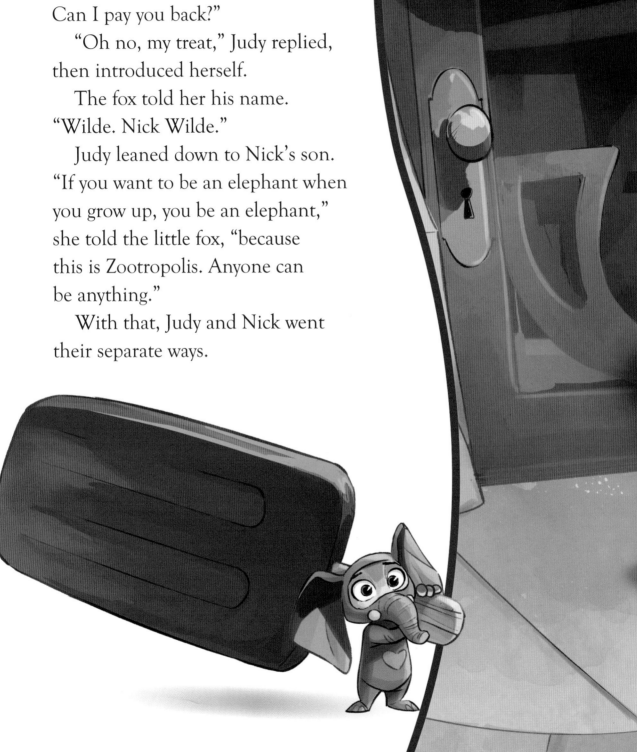

Judy continued with her work, writing up parking tickets all over the city. Then suddenly, she spotted Nick Wilde and his son in the distance. She moved closer to say hello, but stopped when she saw what they were doing.... They were melting the Jumbo-pop and collecting the syrup in jugs!

She watched as the two foxes used the Jumbo-pop juice to make hundreds of little paw-shaped ice pops called pawpsicles, then sold them to lemmings.

Nick was making a lot of money, and the little fox wasn't really his son – he was an adult fox and Nick's partner in crime!

LEMMING BROTHERS BANK

Furious, Judy confronted Nick. "I stood up for you, and you lied to me!"

"It's called a hustle, sweetheart," Nick calmly replied.

Judy tried to arrest Nick, but he pointed out he hadn't actually done anything illegal. He told her she'd never be a real cop.

"Everyone comes to Zootropolis thinking they can be anything they want," Nick said. "Well, you can't. You can only be what you are."

Nick pointed to himself and said, "Sly fox." Then he pointed to
Judy and said, "Dumb bunny."

Judy gasped. "I am not a dumb bunny!"

"Right. And that's not wet cement," Nick replied.

Judy looked down. She had walked right into wet cement and now
she was stuck! As Nick walked off, all Judy could do was watch him go.

The next day at work, Judy was fed up. She wanted to be a real cop! She was issuing another parking ticket when suddenly she heard shouting.

"My shop!" cried a frantic pig. "It just got robbed!"

Judy sprang into action – this was her chance! She raced after the thief, Duke Weaselton, who was carrying a big bag on his shoulder. He was heading towards Little Rodentia and Judy was right behind him.

"I got this one!" Judy called out to another officer. "I am in pursuit!"
She was the only cop small enough to slip into Little Rodentia,
where the tiniest animals in the city lived.
The weasel raced away, stepping on cars and toppling buildings.

When Judy got close, Duke grabbed a huge sign in the shape of a doughnut and threw it at her! Luckily, Judy caught the doughnut just in time. Then she turned and plopped it over Duke's head – he was under arrest!

Back at the ZPD, Judy didn't get the praise she was hoping for. Instead, Chief Bogo was angry with her for abandoning her traffic-warden duties. He said the weasel had only been stealing mouldy onions, but Judy knew they were flower bulbs.

Suddenly, an otter came storming in.

"My husband has been missing for ten days!" the otter exclaimed.

Judy saw her chance. "I will find him!"

Before Bogo could turn Judy down, Assistant Mayor Bellwether arrived. Bogo didn't want Judy to take the case, but Assistant Mayor Bellwether insisted.

Bellwether turned to Judy and winked. "Us little guys really need to stick together."

Chief Bogo was furious that he'd been forced to give Judy a real case, so he gave her only 48 hours to find the missing otter, Emmitt Otterton. If she failed, she would have to resign from the ZPD.

Judy was given the Otterton file, but there wasn't much information. She studied a blurry photo of the otter's last known sighting ... and then looked again. In the photograph, Emmitt was buying an ice pop from Nick Wilde. Maybe the fox knew something!

Judy tracked Nick down. Then, using a hidden microphone in her carrot-shaped pen, she recorded him admitting that he didn't pay tax. To avoid jail and get that pen, Nick agreed to help – for 48 hours only.

Nick took Judy to the last place he had seen Emmitt – a health spa. There they met a yak called Yax, who remembered the licence plate of the car Emmitt had left in....

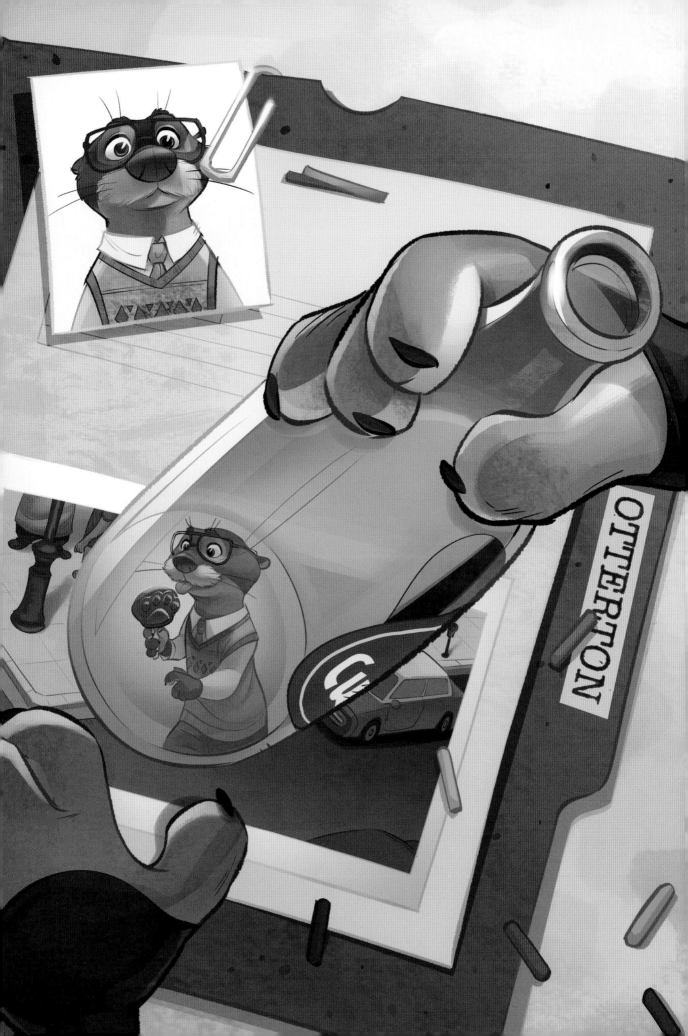

Judy needed to track down that car, but because Judy was new on the force she couldn't access the ZPD system yet. Luckily, Nick had a buddy called Flash at the Department of Mammal Vehicles.

Nick and Judy jumped the queue and Judy gave Flash the licence number: "29THD03."

"Two." Flash typed. "Nine...." Like all the DMV employees, Flash was a sloth – and moved very, very slowly!

To make things worse, Nick told a joke and made Flash laugh very slowly for a very long time! They finally learned that the car belonged to a limousine service in Tundratown, but by now it was dark outside!

Judy was angry with Nick. "You wasted the day on purpose!"

When Judy and Nick tracked down the car, they found Emmitt's wallet on the floor and the seats covered in claw marks! They discovered that the driver who picked up Emmitt had been a jaguar called Manchas, who lived in the Rainforest District. They travelled up into the trees to talk to him.

Manchas turned out to be a frightened jaguar who had been badly beaten by the otter.

"He was down on all fours, a savage," Manchas shuddered. "There was no warning. He just kept yelling about 'night howlers'."

Suddenly Manchas turned, crouched ... and leaped at Judy and Nick!
"Run," said Judy. "RUN!"

The jaguar charged after them, chasing them across slippery branches.
Judy frantically radioed headquarters for help.

Manchas almost chomped Nick, but Judy handcuffed the jaguar's leg
to a post just in time. Thrashing, the big cat knocked Nick and Judy off
their feet and they fell, only just catching themselves among the leaves
before they hit the ground.

When Bogo and the other police officers arrived, Manchas was gone. Judy wasn't sure what had happened to the jaguar, but she told Bogo she was sure this was much more than a missing-mammal case.

"Mr Otterton didn't just disappear," she explained. "I believe he and this jaguar – they went savage!"

"This isn't the Stone Age," Bogo scoffed. "Animals don't go savage." He told Judy to resign, saying they'd made a deal and the bunny had failed to crack the case.

Then Nick interrupted. He reminded Bogo that Judy was given 48 hours to find Otterton and she still had 10 left.

"So if you'll excuse us," Nick said, "we have a very big lead to follow."

Bogo and the other officers stared in disbelief as Nick and Judy stepped onto a passing gondola and floated away.

Judy was touched by Nick's kindness, and Nick admitted that he admired Judy's determination. Bit by bit, they were becoming friends.

Then, Nick had an idea – the city's traffic cameras would have recorded whatever happened to Manchas! They asked Assistant Mayor Bellwether to help them access the camera footage.

Bellwether had to run an errand for the mayor, so Nick and Judy were left alone. Soon they found what they were looking for. The video showed Manchas being picked up by a pack of wolves in a van!

"Night howlers!" Judy exclaimed. "The wolves are the night howlers!"

Nick and Judy worked out that the van had driven to an isolated building at the edge of the city. They went there and sneaked inside.

Judy used the light on her phone to look around one of the dark rooms. She and Nick gasped as they saw fifteen snarling, savage animals – including Manchas and Otterton – all locked in cages!

"All the missing mammals are right here!" Judy gasped.

Hearing someone approach, Nick and Judy hid. They were shocked to see Mayor Lionheart! Judy took out her phone and began recording the mayor's conversation with a doctor.

"We may need to consider their biology, sir," the doctor said. He noted that all the savage animals had something in common and it was getting harder to keep things a secret. "What does Chief Bogo think?"

"Chief Bogo doesn't know," Lionheart replied. "And we are going to keep it that way."

Just then, Judy's phone rang – her parents were calling!

"Sir, you can't be seen!" the doctor told the startled mayor.
He hurried Lionheart away as he yelled, "Help! Security!"

Nick and Judy rushed to escape as the security wolves gave chase.
There seemed to be no way out, except –

"Can you swim?" Judy asked Nick. She was staring at a huge
hippo toilet. With nowhere else to go, they jumped down the drain
... and were dumped out of the building.

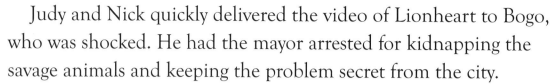

Judy and Nick quickly delivered the video of Lionheart to Bogo, who was shocked. He had the mayor arrested for kidnapping the savage animals and keeping the problem secret from the city.

After that, Bellwether became mayor and Judy became famous! Waiting backstage at a press conference, Judy told Nick that she hoped he would become a police officer. They could be partners! She even finally gave him the recording of him on the carrot pen – she trusted him now.

But Nick's smile faded as Judy told the reporters that the only animals who were going savage were predators. And no one had yet worked out what caused the change ... or if it would happen again.

Nick was furious. He knew this would cause trouble for predators in the city. "It's probably best if you don't have a predator as a partner," he told Judy bitterly. He gave her the police application and strode away.

Over the next few months, all over Zootropolis, animals were no longer getting along. After years of living in harmony, prey animals didn't want to be around predators. They were afraid a normal, friendly predator might turn savage at any moment!

Judy was heartbroken. "I came here to make the world a better place," she said, "but ... I think broke it."

She resigned from the force and headed back to Bunnyburrow

But one day soon after, back at the farm, Judy heard someone yell at a young bunny to avoid the 'night howlers' because their pollen had a strange effect on animals. Judy suddenly realized that night howlers were flowers ... not wolves at all!

"The flowers are making the predators go savage," Judy said to herself. "That's it! That's what I've been missing!"

She jumped straight into the family's truck and drove back to the city. She had to get back on the case!

But first Judy had to find Nick. He was living under a bridge in the city.

"Night howlers aren't wolves. They're toxic flowers," she said, excited. "Someone is targeting predators on purpose and making them go savage!"

Nick shrugged and walked away. Judy realized she owed him an apology.

"I was ignorant and irresponsible," she said humbly. "I really am just a dumb bunny."

Grinning, Nick emerged from the darkness, holding Judy's carrot pen. He had recorded her admitting to being a dumb bunny!

"Cheer up," he said, smiling. "I'll let you erase it in 48 hours."

Nick and Judy were a team again! They jumped into the truck and Nick munched on blueberries from the Hopps farm while Judy started driving.

Judy remembered that the weasel she arrested back in Little Rodentia had been stealing night howler bulbs. There had to be a link! She and Nick tracked down the thief, who told them about a 'drop-spot' for the bulbs in an abandoned underground train station.

At the station, Nick and Judy found a train carriage full of growing night howlers! They watched as a group of rams turned the plant's pollen into little blue pellets and loaded them into a dart gun. This was how someone was turning innocent animals into savages!

Judy knew she had to get the evidence to the ZPD. As soon as they had a chance, she and Nick sneaked into the train carriage and locked the rams out. As the rams tried to break back in, Nick and Judy started the train. But the rams wouldn't give up. While they fought to regain control of the carriage, it sped round a corner and came off the rails!

Nick and Judy jumped out just before the carriage exploded in flames! Luckily, Nick had grabbed a case, with a dart gun and pellets inside, as he escaped – they had their evidence.

Nick and Judy ran towards the ZPD, taking
a shortcut through the empty Natural History
Museum, when suddenly somebody blocked their
path. It was Mayor Bellwether with two huge rams!

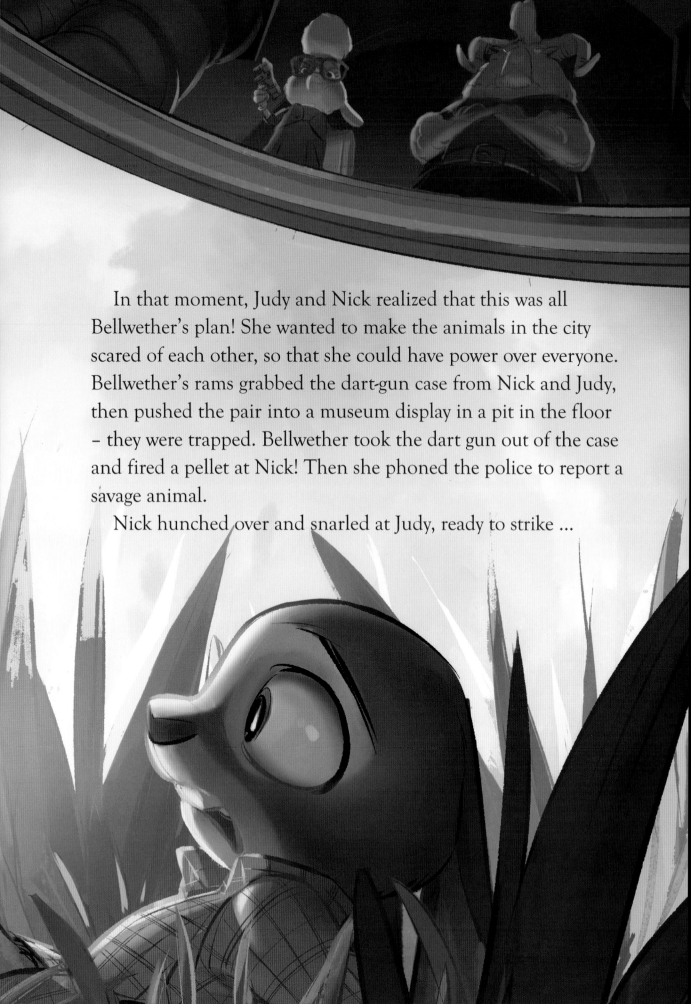

In that moment, Judy and Nick realized that this was all Bellwether's plan! She wanted to make the animals in the city scared of each other, so that she could have power over everyone. Bellwether's rams grabbed the dart-gun case from Nick and Judy, then pushed the pair into a museum display in a pit in the floor – they were trapped. Bellwether took the dart gun out of the case and fired a pellet at Nick! Then she phoned the police to report a savage animal.

Nick hunched over and snarled at Judy, ready to strike ...

"You think if prey fear predators, you'll stay in power?" Judy called desperately to Bellwether. "It won't work!"

"Fear always works." Bellwether smirked. "And I'll dart every predator in Zootropolis to keep it that way."

Suddenly Nick stood up and smiled. He wasn't really going savage! He and Judy had taken the serum out of the gun and replaced it with blueberries! They had also recorded Bellwether's entire confession on the carrot pen.

"It's called a hustle, sweetheart," Judy told Bellwether.

Just then, Bogo and the rest of the ZPD burst onto the scene and arrested Bellwether.

Lionheart was released, though he would have to pay for trying to cover up the scandal. Bellwether, on the other hand, went straight to jail.

Zootropolis began to recover. Prey no longer feared predators, and predators were treated fairly once again. Plus, doctors discovered a cure for the predators who had been infected with the night howler toxin, so Mrs Otterton finally got her husband back.

Best of all, Judy returned to the police force – and Nick joined, too!

At last, Judy and Nick became real partners on the force.

"Still believe it?" Nick asked Judy as they sat in their patrol car.

"That anyone can be anything?" Judy replied. "Mmm, yeah, I do. Even if it's not quite as simple as all that. But the thing is, we'll never know what we can be or what's possible if we don't try."

"Spoken like a true trier," said Nick.

"Takes one to know one," Judy replied with a smile.

Suddenly a red sports car sped past them. Judy started the car and Nick switched on the siren. It was time to fight some crime!

The End